T0107213

ETERNAL MONDAY

Györgi Petri (1943-2000) was a leading Hungarian poet, writer, translator. He studied Hungarian literature and philosophy at Eötvös Loránd University. From 1975 to 1988 his works were banned; his poetry appeared only in samizdat and abroad. Between 1981 and 1989 he was editor of the samizdat newspaper *Beszélő*. After the regime change he became member of the editorial board of the cultural monthly *Holmi*. He was one of the founders of the Digital Literary Academy. Bloodaxe published two editions of his poetry translated by George Gömöri and Clive Wilmer, *Night Song of the Personal Shadow: Selected Poems* (1991) and *Eternal Monday: New & Selected Poems* (1999).

GYÖRGY PETRI

Eternal Monday

NEW & SELECTED POEMS

translated by
CLIVE WILMER
& GEORGE GÖMÖRI

foreword by
ELAINE FEINSTEIN

BLOODAXE BOOKS

Copyright © György Petri 1971, 1974, 1982, 1985, 1991, 1996
Translations copyright © Clive Wilmer & George Gömöri 1991, 1999

ISBN: 978 1 85224 504 7

First published 1999 by
Bloodaxe Books Ltd,
Eastburn,
South Park,
Hexham,
Northumberland NE46 1BS.

www.bloodaxebooks.com
For further information about Bloodaxe titles
please visit our website and join our mailing list
or write to the above address for a catalogue.

Supported using public funding by
**ARTS COUNCIL
ENGLAND**

LEGAL NOTICE
All rights reserved. No part of this book may be
reproduced, stored in a retrieval system, or
transmitted in any form, or by any means, electronic,
mechanical, photocopying, recording or otherwise,
without prior written permission from Bloodaxe Books Ltd.
Requests to publish work from this book
must be sent to Bloodaxe Books Ltd.
György Petri and Clive Wilmer & George Gömöri
asserted their rights under Section 77 of the
Copyright, Designs and Patents Act 1988 to be
identified as author and translators respectively of this work.

This translation was supported by the Frankfurt '99
Programme Office of the Hungarian Ministry of Culture.

Digital reprint of the 1999 Bloodaxe Books edition.

Acknowledgements

Twenty of these translations have been chosen from our earlier selection of Petri's work, *Night Song of the Personal Shadow* (Bloodaxe Books, 1991). Five of them – 'I Am Stuck, Lord, on Your Hook', 'Sweetness', 'In Memoriam: Péter Hajnóczy', 'Christmas 1956' and 'Cold Peace' – have been very slightly revised.

Some of the new translations first appeared in the following periodicals, to whose editors thanks are due: *Hungarian Quarterly, London Magazine, Metre, Poetry Wales, The Spectator, Stand, Times Literary Supplement.* 'Daydreams' has also been published in Clive Wilmer's *Selected Poems* (Carcanet, 1995) and *The Colonnade of Teeth: Modern Hungarian Poetry,* edited by George Gömöri and George Szirtes (Bloodaxe Books, 1996).

The poems are selected from *Magyarázatok M. számára* (Explanations for M., 1971), *Körülírt zuhanás* (Circumscribed Fall, 1974), *Örökhétfő* (Eternal Monday, 1982), *Azt hiszik...* (What They Think, 1985) and *Petri György Versei* (György Petri's Poems, 1996), by kind permission of the author and Jelenkor Publishers. The Hungarian texts of 'The Great Journey' and 'A Recognition' were published in the magazine *Holmi*.

Contents

FOREWORD

The richness of Hungarian poetry survives admirably in translation, as I discovered on my first visit to Budapest in 1976, when many volumes in English were pressed into my hands. I was fortunate enough then to meet Sándor Weöres, speak over lunch with Ágnes Nemes Nagy, and talk through a long evening with János Pilinszky in the confusion of his dusty, crowded apartment. There were many great poets I could not meet of course; Miklós Radnóti, for instance, shot dead in 1944 on a forced march, with a notebook of poems miraculously preserved in his raincoat. But György Petri I *could* have met. He was not yet an unperson; indeed his first books of poetry had been published with official approval (or at least permission) in 1971 and 1974. Unfortunately, I did not know his name.

A generation younger than Zbigniew Herbert and Miroslav Holub, Petri shares many of their strengths: an inventive use of image, irony, a subtle awareness of the absurdities of the human condition. Like them, he had to learn how far he could go in challenging authority. A selection from his early books, in which he managed that balancing act with great skill, forms the first section of this volume. It was not until 1981, when Petri was told that 30 poems had to be cut from a new book before it could be published, that he turned his back on official success and began to publish in *samizdat*. That is how the poems in the second section first appeared.

Like the countries on its borders, Hungary has had a desperate history, occupied brutally first by their German allies, then by the Russians who put down an uprising with great savagery in 1956. By the time a visitor arrived in Hungary in the seventies, however, Budapest had the air of being a staging-post to the West; Váci Street was elegant, there were well-dressed women, and it no longer had the depressed, poverty-stricken air of other countries in the Eastern bloc. This relative prosperity came from the astuteness of the Communist Party leader János Kádár and, though he had long since abandoned his economic reforms, it was at least a high point of Hungarian publishing, which subsidised both local poets and European poets in translation with great generosity.

There was little real freedom of expression, however, for all the signs of material well-being; hence Petri's epigram about inspecting the laces in his shoes to confirm he is not literally imprisoned.

> I glance down at my shoe and – there's the lace!
> This can't be gaol then, can it, in that case?

9

Under Communism, poetry was powerful; it was widely read, because what could not be said openly could be recognised in a hint there. Petri felt he had a responsibility to comment on the society around him, and mocked both rulers and ruled as well as the system itself.

His tone is not that of Holub or Herbert, though his situation is comparable. He is altogether less civilised, more savage than amused, less indignant than disgusted. He presents himself not as a sophisticated observer, amused by human weakness and stupidity, but as a rogue, an outsider, a Villon born to be hanged, repelled equally by the tricks of those in power and the collective idiocy of those they rule. He turns the same withering contempt on his own behaviour, particularly his self-indulgent idleness. Even as he muses 'It would be nice to translate Mallarmé', he imagines an escape to a cruise liner where he could travel first-class, and sit on a deck-chair with no debts or dependants. His 'omnivorous greed' for life is a hair's breadth away from boredom. In the title-poem 'Eternal Monday' bewildered organisers of such matters are assured that whatever they may think to the contrary *'there is a day going on all the time'*; they settle on a surreal view not dissimilar from Lewis Carroll's: if so, 'it must have been yesterday'.

Since Petri always read the political world through images of sex and death, the astonishing events of 1989, which saw the clamps of Communism removed from the whole of Eastern Europe at a stroke, did not destroy his material as a satirist. The poems in the third section of this book explore, among other things, how late capitalism makes itself felt in Budapest. Even having a bank account is a new experience – Petri never had a steady job under Communism – and he records the 55,000 *forints* that remain on the eighth of the month with an ironic boastfulness. He admits to a certain nostalgia for Soviet-produced *Stolichnaya Vodka,* and to visiting Moscow, where he feels at home in a pub. Crucially, he confesses his continuing inner sense of 'nothing going on' even when there is sunshine and a golden-haired 'lady' at his side.

Petri offers no consolatory belief to reduce the threat of the blood clot 'swimming towards his heart', and though he writes defiantly that he has no wish to return as a Stone Guest, his fear of extinction is palpable. In one of the rare, affectionate poems in this book, he recalls the dead poet István Vas, that lovely singer of the streets of Budapest, and reflects sadly that while Vas's work will survive, the man who drank red wine and smoked cigars is gone forever.

Petri's brooding reflections will find an instant echo in Western readers in this last year of the century:

> I did have a want once, one shared with others.
> I don't want anything now.

As readers of this remarkable selection of poems will discover to their delight, György Petri is an entirely individual voice, wonderfully served here by his translators.

ELAINE FEINSTEIN

INTRODUCTION

György Petri, who was born in 1943, is regarded by many of his fellow-Hungarians as the most original poet of his generation. Some would also say he is the best: high praise in a country which, in the 20th century alone, has produced such poets as Attila József, Miklós Radnóti, Sándor Weöres and János Pilinszky. Petri has always spoken respectfully of his illustrious forebears and acknowledged the greatness of the tradition he was born to. Nevertheless, he has decisively turned his back on many of its most characteristic methods.

Hungarian Modernism, unlike its English counterpart, frankly admits to roots in Romanticism. Petri has discarded the rhetoric of the Romantics in favour of a language that is harsh, spare, colloquial and ironic. He eschews overt attempts at idealism, pathos or beauty; what grips us in his poetry is its force and uncompromising truthfulness, which spares nothing – not even his own posture as truth-teller. As he says in a poem on the murder of Imre Nagy (who led the revolutionary government of 1956), 'My eyes are dry. I need them for looking with.'

As those lines suggest, he is not a consoling writer. He has the knack of antagonising those whose status depends on illusions. He suffered many years of privation during the Communist era, when he refused to compromise with state censorship. Just recently, he was attacked by a conservative Deputy in the Hungarian Parliament, who denounced the poem 'Apocryphal' as blasphemous and a national disgrace. This is not to say that he is unappreciated. Since 1989, he has been honoured frequently and praised for his courage in resisting the dictatorship. Yet he remains an awkward customer. That fact, set in the context of his country's change in direction, gives this choice of his poems its distinctive character.

What Petri most obviously shares with his Romantic forebears is the assumption that poetry cannot avoid politics. The history of Hungary has mostly been the history of its subjection to mightier powers. For a person born, as Petri was, in Budapest in 1943, this truism has been more than usually self-evident. At that time Hungary, though formally independent, was in practice an ally of the Axis powers and, somewhat reluctantly, subject to German policy. In March 1944, illusion gave way to brute fact when the German army occupied the country. Thirteen months later it was liberated by the Russians. A democratic government was elected but by 1948 the Communists had effectively taken over. They set about securing their position and that of their Soviet patrons by removing all opposition to their rule – including that of some fellow-Communists who felt less than subservient to the Soviet Union.

The darkest years of dictatorship were the early 1950s, when even a poet as unpolitical as Sándor Weöres was unable to publish freely: this is the period ironically commemorated in Petri's poem 'By an Unknown Poet from Eastern Europe, 1955'. The date in the title is there in part to remind us of what was soon to follow. 1956 was the year of the brief, glorious and doomed uprising, which brought the evils of Stalinism to world attention. On 23 October 1956, Imre Nagy, a Communist of liberal and patriotic sympathies, was summoned by popular acclaim to free the country from foreign domination. But on the 24th, Russian troops entered Budapest and met with stiff resistance. A brief armistice followed, and for a few euphoric days, it seemed as though the popular will would hold. But on 4 November, in Petri's words, Budapest 'woke to gunfire/that blew it apart'. The uprising was quickly crushed and Nagy arrested. Then, in June 1958, he was tried for treason *in camera* and secretly hanged.

All this is necessary background to Petri's tribute 'To Imre Nagy' and his poetic memoir 'Christmas 1956', which hints at the role played by those tragic events in what Wordsworth called 'the growth of a poet's mind'. For the next 33 years – the years of Petri's adolescence and young manhood – Hungarian politics was dominated by the quisling János Kádár, the 'Aegisthus, with his trainee-barber's face', who makes love to Clytemnestra (Mother Hungary) in Petri's version of the Electra story.

Kádár was a paradoxical figure. Implicated in the Soviet invasion and the beneficiary of Nagy's removal, he used his credit with the Soviet Union to introduce a measure of liberal reform. As a result, by the 1970s, the country was much the most prosperous in the Soviet bloc and politically the most relaxed. This was 'goulash Communism': a system based on half-truths, nods and winks. Petri loathed and despised it. It would not be an exaggeration to say that it largely determined the character of his mature poetry. It turned a man with the talents of a lyrical poet into a formidably trenchant satirist. The Hungarian dictatorship, he told me in an interview, was 'more sophisticated... more clever' than the other Communist governments.* This made it, in Petri's eyes, more contemptible.

* The interview, also quoted elsewhere in this introduction, was published in Clive Wilmer, *Poets Talking: The 'Poet of the Month' Interviews from BBC Radio 3* (Manchester: Carcanet, 1994).

The control it exerted by these subtle means went deeper, so 'the moral state of the people' was more dangerously corrupted. As the tone here indicates, Petri – despite his penchant for flippancy and obscenity – is as rigorous a moralist as Jonathan Swift.

The superficiality of Kádár's liberalism and the opportunistic dishonesty of goulash Communism were exposed when in 1968 the Hungarian army took part in the Warsaw Pact invasion of Czechoslovakia. The Prague government's economic reforms bore some resemblance to Kádár's own, though politically and morally Alexander Dubček was by contrast a genuine liberal. For young intellectuals like Petri, most of them more or less Marxist despite their opposition to the Soviet hegemony, this was the last straw. By 1981, when martial law was imposed on Poland with the tacit assent of the Kádár regime, an unofficial opposition had begun to develop in Hungary. Petri became committed to this movement and, like most of its activists, joined the radically liberal Alliance of Free Democrats (SDS) when the system collapsed in 1989.

In 1990 I interviewed Petri in Budapest. It was the week of Hungary's first free general election since the end of the Second World War. He was guardedly optimistic. Before 1989, he said, to write political poetry had been 'a moral obligation, because [under Communism] there was no normal canalisation for the expression of political opinion'. The advent of democracy meant for him personally 'that I am not obliged to participate in political life any more...I hope that I will have the opportunity to be a dissident in another meaning of the word.' And he went on as follows:

> In a totalitarian system political life is over-dramatised. One can say that political life is very poetic. In a normal democracy the political life is very prosaic...and boring! I hope that we are now beginning to live with a boring political life! I never feel...an obligation or *engagement*. For me, politics, the political life, was a theme, a *motif*, and I was engaged in political activities as a man, but not as a poet. I was concerned in a lot of my poetry with politics, but because it was interesting, because it was dramatic...but now everything's changed.

Events in some parts of the former Communist bloc have been less prosaic, perhaps, than Petri was hoping. Some have been simply tragic. He was, when he spoke to me, aware of such dangers but, by and large, his hopes for the future of Hungary were more or less realistic. The comments I have quoted include some playful posturing, but they are strangely accurate in their anticipation of the changes that were to take place in his poetry. He has had to discover new themes and new dramas, but he remains 'a dissident in another meaning of the word'. Still more revealing is what these remarks imply about his earlier poems and the personae who speak in them. Petri is a major political poet but he was never one by choice. Quite as much as Heaney, Mahon and Longley on our own end of the map, he was forced into political utterance by the circumstances of his daily life and found there was matter to relish in it. It gave his language something to chew upon.

Whatever his political commitments, therefore, he was never a partisan but, essentially and instinctively, an anarchist, a loner, a questioner of authority. Long before it seemed likely that the Soviet system would collapse, Western critics were given to wondering how Eastern dissidents would appear in literary terms if their most compelling subject disappeared. In the last poem in this book Petri registers that challenge:

> The epoch expired like a monstrous predator.
> My favourite toy's been snatched.

The note of lament there is not wholly ironical.

This book is divided into three sections. The first consists of poems from Petri's first two books, published in 1971 and 1974 by a state publishing house. Though Petri's concerns at this time were mostly philosophical, one does not have to read the poems closely to notice some fierce criticism of the Communist state. But the Kádár regime at this time preferred not to notice such things and, when they were not graphically signposted, managed to ignore them. This was the dishonesty that so disgusted Petri, who realised that it was not a genuine liberalism – that any freedom granted in this way could be instantly withdrawn. (This is the burden of his splendid epigram 'To Be Said Over and Over Again'.)

Such apparent freedom, however, had advantages. In those years, official recognition by the state could bring a writer prestige and privilege of a kind unknown in the capitalist world. In 1981 Petri turned his back on such advantages. On submitting a new book for publication, he was informed that several of the poems were politically unacceptable, though if they were cut the book could still be published. He refused, and the following year the book appeared in *samizdat*. Section two of this book represents the *samizdat* collections of 1982 and 1985. Section three is made up of poems published – though not always written – in the years since 1989, when it became possible for Petri to publish legally again. His *Collected Poems* appeared in 1996.

Of the 56 translations in this selection, 20 first appeared in an earlier book, *Night Song of the Personal Shadow*, published by

Bloodaxe in 1991. Despite this overlap, I suspect that readers will find the new book different in character. This is partly because of the 'post-Communist' poems, but also because in the new context the earlier poems acquire some different perspectives.

Most obviously, many of the political poems share a tone with those that are almost self-consciously post-modern and irresponsible. One sees, too, how personal they often are. The poem 'Night Song of the Personal Shadow', for instance, though it stands as an indictment of the Kádár regime for its persecution of independent thinkers, is on the imaginative plane a half-sympathetic study of an alter ego, who shares the poet's smouldering discontent. More immediately, though, it is a simple act of revenge. As a dissident writer Petri was shadowed for a period and, in this portrait of the secret policeman as archetypal bigot and state parasite, he gets his own back. In much the same spirit, his Electra's desire for the death of Clytemnestra has nothing to do with love of Agamemnon or even moral principle. It is 'Because of disgust, because it all sticks in my craw'. To take a slightly different perspective, 'Collapse', written in the acceptable code of the 1970s, is really about the decay from within of the Communist system – it is in that sense startlingly prophetic – but when we set it against the more "personal" poem that follows it, 'You Are Knackered, My Catullus', we may notice some odd similarities. The second poem is, half-humorously, about the persona's impulse to self-destruction, to interior decay. The same theme is still in evidence in a poem from the late 1990s, 'The Great Journey', where personal dissipation is explicitly set in a context of political collapse, the disintegration of the Soviet Union. The one concern is analogous to the other and there is nothing to tell which is primary.

In my introduction to *Night Song of the Personal Shadow*, I appeared to stress the political at the expense of the personal when I praised Petri as a satirist. My emphasis was questioned by George Szirtes. 'Petri,' he wrote in an interesting review, 'is a lyrical poet who has deliberately gone sour... His love poems are his finest work: sad, dry-eyed, even cruel, but spiced with a bitter tenderness... He shows his love of the passing and corruptible by describing it.' I don't see why being a lyrical poet precludes being a satirist as well, but otherwise this is acute criticism, in particular because it points to the beauty and pathos that lie beyond Petri's rejection of pleasant fancies and rhetorical flourishes. It reminds us, moreover, that love and death, the lyrical poet's perennial subjects, are more central to Petri's work than politics.

Death is as present to Petri as it might be to a medieval poet surrounded by images of mortality. It defines whatever it is we call identity by drawing a line around it. It is as if the ghost in the machine only became a person once the machine had collapsed. This is a characteristically modern problem and it makes itself felt most insistently in the poems about love. For if personality seems so arbitrary and fragmented, what does that make of the constancy that love is said to require? These questions contribute a note of cynicism to Petri's poems and particularly to his love poems, which one is tempted to reclassify as 'sex poems'. But it is precisely this cynicism that discloses by implication the unstated tenderness referred to by Szirtes: the pathos of a noble aspiration that seems to terminate in the manoeuvres of finite bodies.

What this shows, I think, is how much of Petri's meaning lies beyond his actual language. Paradoxically this means that, on first reading, his language is more opaque than we expect. It is not transparent to the subject that lies behind it. This presents serious problems to the translator, for a great deal of Petri's recent poetry – especially that which is free of politics – depends on word-play and linguistic puzzles, all of which are simply untranslatable. This means, too, that the poems in Section three are those we felt we were able to translate rather than those we thought precisely the best – though some of them are surely among the best. It also means that Petri's subject-matter is often elusively tenuous in a way that seemed less the case when he had an enemy to focus on.

Yet in such poems as 'Daydreams', 'Ideas and Dance-Music Records', 'Our Loves' and 'The Great Journey', he remains a dazzling poet: by turns, coarse, desolate, funny, poignant and clear-sighted. If he has arisen from the special circumstances of the former Communist bloc, he increasingly seems a citizen of the world, a poet who looks at reality with a courage that, maybe, all of us now have to learn. As he says in 'Smiley's Christmas':

> All that can save us now, all that can save,
> is absolute distrust

– though reading between the lines, one cannot feel the distrust to be something he wholly welcomes.

CLIVE WILMER

I

TO 1974

Collapse

No, there was no explosion.
Just a collapse.
Crumbling away on the inside,
deluding itself while deceiving others,
it terrorised through appearances
and fell apart noiselessly.

Can you still contemplate...

eaten up by doubt from the outset,
giving up even the right to doubt,
can the idiotic guardian of stale bathwater –
water in which
was there even a baby, you can't tell –
can he contemplate liberation?

Can anybody imagine such a thing –
watching it fall noiselessly apart,
softlier
than bodies after love,
softlier than, one day, flesh from bone?

Just slid apart noiselessly,
nails slipping softly through spongey beams,
the bricks like clay or potash,
their porous dryness yielding, bonding
debased, no reason to resist.
Shrapnel hammers the earth, round on round:
a laughable supremacy
hammering vacant air
like rain, rain, rain.

No, there was no explosion: just a collapse.
And it took time, a very long time,
for the thick, dampened dust
to settle down, grain jostling grain.
So is that all there is to it, this jostling?
This wet bulge, barging about?

The constructed world falling apart.

You Are Knackered, My Catullus

You are knackered, my Catullus, you wake with a skull
heavy as stone, your feet tight bags of water.
As for your mirror, better not look. Not all of Rome's
most refined balsams would restore your slack and pallid skin.
And your teeth, too, teeth that were once so white! –
that's how a city-wall, once ruined, turns to decay.
Where now are the days of 'ready for nine embraces in one go'?
Your used-up body, the yawning silent sum of all of this,
does not tell to what extent the causes of this effect
were a great passion, exemplary for centuries,
and ceaseless, omnivorous greed –
how much due to the poison of deliciously high living
and how much to the stewed gut-rot of low taverns.

By an Unknown Poet from Eastern Europe, 1955

It's fading,
        like the two flags that, year by year,
we'd put out for public holidays
in the iron sheaths stuck over the gate –
like them the world's looking pale, it's fading now.

Where have they gone, the days of pomp and cheer?

Smothered with dust
in the warmth
of an attic room,
a world dismantled holds its peace.

The march has gone and disappeared.

It metamorphosed into a howl
the wind winnowed.
And now, instead of festive poets here,
the wind will recite into thin air,

it will utter scurrying dust and pulsating heat
above the concrete square.

That our women have been loved seems quite incredible.

Above the era
of taut ropes and white-hot foundries,
the tentative, wary
present – dust settling – hovers.

Above unfinished buildings:
imperial frauds, fantasies.

I no longer believe
what I believed once.
But the fact that I have believed –
that I compel myself
day by day to recall.

And I do not forgive anyone.

Our terrible loneliness
crackles and flakes
like the rust on iron rails in the heat of the sun.

To a Virtuous Lady

Trousers are indisputably progressive,
something attained: a triumph of the spirit.
Trousers ennoble
the worthy and the chosen.
Being both categorical and imperative,
their legs are, in a sense,
historical preconditions of cleanliness.
Though sometimes, in our folly, we think to drop them,
it's only a textile coating of the world
falls to the ground: for trousers
are virtually impossible to shed.

But because our coupling species, with its lust,
learns morals and mores only lazily,
nostalgically glancing back at savage custom,
we permit for the time being –
to relieve the iron discipline of trousers –
a discreet opening for the love lyric.

No more of this. Lady, give me your hand!
Place it upon my brow! I may calm down.
You see, I am not yet perfect;
but disregard the slightest of my foibles
and you preserve the discipline.

So help me and together we, perhaps,
may rise to a subtler irony:
that of the wise man who can't help but giggle
when he's touched unexpectedly –
because his skin, that sensitive guinea-pig,
is tickled by the spirit.

I Am Stuck, Lord, on Your Hook

I am stuck, Lord, on your hook.
I've been wriggling there, curled up,
for the past twenty-six years
alluringly, and yet
the line has never gone taut.
It's now clear
there are no fish in your river.
Lord, if you still have hopes,
choose some other worm. Being
among the elect
has been beautiful. All the same,
what I'd just like to do, right now,
is dry off and loll about in the sun.

News Bulletin

As dust in a crook of the stairs coagulates,
softly the dirt of the age accumulates.

Stairs

Who was it invented
circumscribed fall
– stairs,
which tame height, the frozen
perpendicular melted
down to degrees; and –
the cunning of the solution –
showed wingless man
the modest trick
of the detour, when he'd
try to jump
in vain after his glance?

To S.V.

The bus was taking me
over the bridge and I looked
on into the tunnel. At
the far end of that pipe
padded with shadows, there were
vehicles hanging about –
quarantined
in an unreachably distant
sandy sun-strip.

A long time since
we were last watching together –
looking out for occasions
to enrich our occasional
poetry with occasions of pain.
Filing away at lyric skeleton-keys
we gauge by sight
for a small circle of friends.

I amble on alone –
the prisoner of a condition it'd be
going too far to call loneliness
and deceiving myself to call independence – on
among parched sights.
I walk down to the embankment looking for shade.
In glass-melting heat
the bus I have just got off
is crawling away somewhere.

An airless tent of chestnuts. But up there
already, the infant stars, as yet
tenderly spiked, herald the autumn.
The water's putrescent slate.
But at least it gets broken up
by a boat putting out from here.
A sight, a view: I've no one
to share it with.
Summer's fruits have ripened
in me and they taste soapy.

I could already tell we were in for a bad year
the morning after New Year's Eve.
In a city of iron shutters, all pulled down,
we dithered about on insidious snow
looking for soak-up soup or hair-of-the-dog.
We ended up drinking iodine-yellow beer
in a surgically tiled café.
And time we stepped outside,
the street was wearing eyesore white.

Our weak brains stop working.
Sailors on ships that are locked in ice,
as is well-known, will devour each other.
Just like the modern Theatre of Provocation –
it all degenerates, banter
into argument, teasing
into insult. Till finally the background
cracks the backbone of the situation.

From the Songs of the Doleful Lover

I'm bored with you, my darling, I am bored!
And that's what I'd like to put across to you
quite churlishly, without room for misunderstanding.
I am now so full of strength and sure conviction
that, were you here,
I really would say this to you.
In the expectant silence
of this beautiful and lonely hour of night...

which is the hour that's dearest to the heart,
that of receding darkness. Or you could call it
sparse light rather,
for in it things are faintly visible.
I listen to the sleeping universe
rumbling away and by fag-light vaguely see
how with the mediation of the wrist
my arm concludes in a gracefully shaped hand.
Or else I take delight in my wristwatch,
that functional, masculine ornament.

Musing like this, I get bored with you day by day
at this hour, this one I steal for myself, in silence.
How could I say to your face that I'm bored? And when?
Perhaps when, powered by your downy, white legs,
a sewing-machine, I move to my own rhythm?
Well, the cult of the Virgin, which
through the forms that proceed from it...
But on my own, I don't always finish sentences
in these intimate little holidays of the soul. No,
I won't say it. Of course not. I won't tell...

though for ten years now, no, more than ten years,
you've set fire to the sugar-wrappers in the ash-tray
at coffee-time. Each of them separately.
And you unfold them first, so they burn longer,
and gawp at them. For the past ten years. That's 3,650 days –
we've had coffee together every afternoon.

Now Only

now only the filthy pattering of rain
now only heavy coats and squelching shoes
now only the din of steamed-up cheap cafés
now only trodden sawdust on the stone

now only mouldy buns in cellophane
now streetlights decomposing in thin fog
the advice given by a friendly cop
the last drink bought with the last of the small change

now only the tram-island's desolation
now only the variable course of the night wind
rushing through a town of alleys to no end

now only the unfinished excavations
the night's prospecting-hole its weeds and thorns
now only shivering now only yawns

Gratitude

The idiotic silence of state holidays
is no different
from that of Catholic Sundays.
People in collective idleness
are even more repellent
than they are when purpose has harnessed them.

Today I will not
in my old ungrateful way
let gratuitous love decay in me.
In the vacuum of streets
what helps me to escape
is the memory of your face and thighs,
your warmth,
the fish-death smell of your groin.

You looked for a bathroom in vain.
The bed was uncomfortable
like a roof ridge.
The mattress smelt of insectide,
the new scent of your body mingling with it.

I woke to a cannonade
(a round number of years ago
something happened). You were still asleep.
Your glasses, your patent leather bag
on the floor, your dress on the window-catch
hung inside out – so practical.

One strap of your black slip
had slithered off.
And a gentle light was wavering
on the downs of your neck, on your collar-bones,
as the cannon went on booming

and on a spring poking through
the armchair's cover
fine dust was trembling.

II

1974 – 1989

Eternal Monday

When Monday –
not only to the vast surprise
of the organisers but, more,
against all their expectations –
successfully took place,
the tiny tots,
who couldn't have remembered
the mounting troubles
of Tuesday, Wednesday and Thursday –
and even the spectacular catastrophe
Friday had been
succeeded in leaving no more of a trace
than "paperbags burst with a bang" –
they began, these tots, to criticise
Saturdays off
and Palm Sunday
(the grown-ups, not even knowing
what day it was,
went along with their age
and, in due accordance with respective age,
one by one kicked the bucket).
It was left to the infants and the nursery kids
to stamp with fury:
Why is it Drum Wednesday,
why Love Thursday, how can poor Teeny Tuesday
turn suddenly into great Good Friday,
how is it that a reasonable border-line
between Silver and Golden Sundays
can be drawn only from the dynamic perspective
of Ash Wednesday, and as for the aptly named
Pancake Tuesday, well,
there was certainly no meat in it – it was not,
at any rate, meat
they left behind.
        The yet-unborn
watched the whole
of this comedy with disgust,
saying that everything in it was pure fiction
so long as they went on talking

about all these thingamijigs, not clearly stating:
Friday lasts longer
than Saturday.

Even after that,
the grown-ups still couldn't tell
what day of the week it was, although
they informed the organisers that, allegedly,
there's a day going on all the time.
The organisers, in their great time-confusion,
were of one view, which was: It's yesterday.
And so they began to experiment
with anniversaries, saying things like
'Today is the 150th year of yesterday'.
Then they changed over
from round numbers to elliptic ones
(Tomorrow is yesterday's 132nd,
and so on) but those in the top infants
as well as the babes in the nursery
and the yet-unborn
and sadly even
the ungrown-ups as well
made obscene gestures
with their chronolollipops
and sand-clocks;
with epoch-making pongs
their farts inflated leaky balloons,
satellites that shat a lot were launched,
their cocksure posters stuck up on the walls,
their trashy banners flashed
and pigs with wings –
all this on the thousand-year-old Momentary Square
where an ad hoc meeting was held
and they kept howling:
What's today? What's today?
Since the introduction of Eternal Monday
at Eternity (formerly Momentary) Square,
thousand-year-old
turfs have flourished green
around tableaux vivants.
Bluebells and harebells
chime out: Monday! Monday!

Only the gardeners looking after graves
keep mumbling to themselves:
Monday, Tuesday, Wednesday,
Thursday, Friday,
Saturday – and setting down their rusty watering-cans
in the sunlit cemetery –
Sunday.

Gloss on a Discussion
(for Sándor Radnóti)

When we weren't actually booted up the bum,
we honoured what was called their "liberalism".
A 'get lost' phrased with flowery circumstance
would turn *Repression* to *Toleranz.*
On this side of the Urals, beyond the Oder,
the self-control régime's arranged by terror.
The confectioner stocks truncheons made of gum –
it's universal pre-consumerism.
If our only pleasure in this is critical,
will "commune" do to label this cramped hole?
When we fuck now, do we just fuck critically,
so long as the *Kultur* masters let us be?
You *made the political sphere transcendent* – but
I, even now, just *keep my mouth shut.*
Things fall apart; too tired for hateful passion,
I only hate your guts in dreamy fashion.
Nebich. Vollendete Sündhaftigkeit!
The future (I hope) will drop us both outright.
It will smell the fact that *alle beide stinken,*
and in the same way everything is linked in
with all, humiliates all. Our base fits
of rage are noble let-outs – they're like farts:
painful no doubt, but also ridiculous...
loves hurt internally just as wind does.
So into the margin I blurt this little note.
My verses cramp like bowels, tensed and taut.

It Would Be Nice to Translate Mallarmé

It would be nice to translate Mallarmé,
but in the mean time I keep musing how
I've always fancied sailing first-class, really,
to gaze at the crumbling waves from a deck-chair
with no debts or dependents. Nevertheless,
I have nothing to eat
and, what's worse at the moment, others feed me
(though this is idle talk – it'd be worse still
if others didn't feed me; this way,
like the vile Balkan pigeons in our courtyard,
I still have everything) but these thoughts distract me
from Mallarmé, though it would be *so* nice
to translate Mallarmé in another life
(other lives being always full of sunshine)
where people translate Mallarmé, not knowing
this world with its grim winters.

Tick-Tock

The stalemate of our love.
Somehow
it will end. It's just that we
don't know how.
I live now through the available variations
of love on offer only in myself.
Having acquired a certain experience
in regard to what our sisters can accomplish
with *that* part of the male anatomy,
I do it in imagination now.

Here, on the bed, lying next to you.

And as any moment of time
is convenient for God to lend his ears to a prayer,
every moment is perfect.

The Fading Consciousness of Casanova

Women
women
in whom I have spent time

a garden hose in the care-
taker's hands

Apocryphal

The holy family's grinding away –
Mary lies back, God screws;
Joseph, unable to sleep,
starts groping about for booze.
No luck: he gets up. Grabs his things.
Over pyjamas pulls vest and pants.
Then walks down to the Three Kings
for (at last!) a couple of pints...
'God again?'
                    'Him again.'
                                        He sighs,
knocks back his beer, gets wise,
gesticulates:
                    'Anyway,
I can tell you, the other day
did I make a fuss: before my very eyes,
the two of 'em on the job!
So I told my Mary straight,
at least shut your gob,
it's enough that the damn bed shakes
and rumbles on as if there was an earthquake.
I mean it now: if he's really got to screw yuh,
I can do without all the ha-ha-ha-hallelujah!'

To Be Said Over and Over Again

I glance down at my shoe and – there's the lace!
This can't be gaol then, can it, in that case.

S.K.

That dead woman
dead fourteen years
a young woman
crosses our room at night
potters about absent-mindedly
ambles in and out of the room
picks up and nicks things I then
can't find in the morning

or just stands up against the wall
and although dead
stares straight ahead in terror
as if facing a firing squad

she begins to undress
takes off the things she had on
when she went
knickers and stockings
and I keep pleading   No
it's impossible   Not here and now

she puts her coat on
over the blue-lace breastplate
and sidling away retreats
as if afraid I might hit her
her "camel-hair" swagger coat
she pulls it over her
shivering
asks me 'Why don't you put the fire on?' and
'Why are you alive?'

The Under-Secretary Makes a Statement

Four special government committees
and five professors of dialectics with them
have been meeting to study the mysterious
rising-power that is inherent in prices.
The hypothesis put forward by the committees
is that prices have a *randy nature*
and whenever they sight a crowd of housewives
sniffing about in jam-packed queues, they instantly
stiffen like furious Don Juans and rise
and no amount of soothing will bring them down –
entreaties only get them more worked up.
As for wages, they have staying power,
so don't go up, although they do stand fast.
The mysterious working committees have so far –
at a hundred and nine working dinners,
three hundred and thirty-seven working lunches
and two hundred and forty working snacks
(what a job it was to gobble that lot up) –
held discussions in thirty different suites
at a total cost of twenty million zlotys
exclusive of all per diem allowances.

But the housewives are impatient –
so many old hags, grannies in particular,
endlessly moaning on about varicose veins
and seeing no further than their carrier bags:
'Meat – meat – meat – meat!' they howl
egging their husbands on to do likewise,
grandpas out on the streets shaking their crutches.
Even the babies wail.

                        We simply cannot
work, there's so much noise. So, housewives,
let us, for the last time, make this appeal
to your sober understandings: either you make
your husbands and babies belt up, or else
we cannot be held responsible
and might be driven to perform such deeds
as you would later on regret yourselves.

The key to the situation is in our hands
and we do not shrink from using it to lock up
whole peoples, if that is what necessity dictates.

Night Song of the Personal Shadow

The rain is pissing down,
you scum.
And you, you are asleep
in your nice warm room –
that or stuffing the bird.
Me? Till six in the morning
I rot in the slackening rain.
I must wait for my relief, I've got to wait
till you crawl out of your hole,
get up from beside your old woman.
So the dope can be passed on
as to where you've flown.
You are flying, spreading your wings.
Don't you get into my hands –
I'll pluck you while you're in flight.
This sodding rain
is something I won't forget,
my raincoat swelling
double its normal weight
and the soles of my shoes.
While you
were arsing around
in the warm room.

The time will come
when I feed you to fish in the Danube.

Sweetness

There is no present   Slowly
I chew on the crystallised past
Syrupy time   I let it
Congeal into sugar

Me

God's only-begotten
rotten grape, the one
the old gent keeps for himself
in the frost-freighted garden.

Horatian

I could bear life in silence, even without a timetable.
I'd withdraw among the chickens and pigs, and do without ideas.
Yet again I'd repair fences, mend broken tiles
and be glad to see the young marrow flowering.

I've no ambition – less than a corpse in a grave
who, tickled by worms, dreams of a deathless tombstone
over his mortal remains.
I have seen and lived enough. I'll spend the short time ahead
in a waiting-room hung with spittle, littered with butts:
eyes open, resting my roaring head
on a dented suitcase.
No newspapers or tobacco or firewater:
there's a broken fag in my pocket still
and syrupy liqueur in a stray bottle.
A tramp lights my fag. Then all my bad dreams
about power and violence I pull up over my head.
I'll dream that I'm a police-dog, my coat shiny.

As I disintegrate into pure reason, I can come to no harm.
Except that trudging a Milky Way gone sour
makes the wounded sole of my spirit gangrenous.
Until that wharf on the River Styx is reached.

Sometimes the Sun Comes Out

Yesterday wafts through today and tomorrow.
The taste of beaten-back desire,
like a worm in a hard green apple, burrows deep:
beneath all our urgencies, failure gnaws.

We all know this – and yet, when in the morning,
a clean shirt on your back, you leave the house
and are glanced at by the well-washed world,
an illusion of perfect knees will penetrate
your numbed and idle senses,
scented hair brushes against your face
and this feminine challenge draws you further in
– offering a beginning, not a continuation!
It says not a word, but fixes you
with a smiling eye, no batting of the lid:
it promises joy, or a torment that's more appropriate.

Black Christmas

I'm forty. I can't tell what will come.
The winter is mild. Not on to the snow,
but on to the coarse, straw-strewn mud
of a grim courtyard, time,
as if from a slashed artery,
ever-diminishing, spurts.

In Memoriam: Péter Hajnóczy

I

My simple, singular, old friend is gone:
not to be seen on this restless earth again.
For earth is jealous and will not submit
to sending back one so much part of it.

II

Forgive me for having troubled you.
(As if anyone'd care
a jot for such scruples over there...)
But of those left here so few

phoning me up would find me
so irritable-anxious for their hello:
I'll never meet such another silken buffalo;
though invariably my life is intertwined

with fluffy news, flimsy messages,
logorrhoeic specimens, supernumeraries,
several "imposing cut-outs", several one-day lays,

and my projects, my pretexts.
Well, rest in peace there: time goes on its way.
That's quite enough rhyming on pain now for one text.

III

I have more and more cravings,
and fewer and fewer days
to tell off to the last one.
By 2030 (a generous estimate)
we shall – with our wives and our enemies,
those who keep eyes on us and those who pant with us –
all of us, all together, all enrich the soil,
the weird deposit bulldozers scoop up out of it.
A child, jubilant, knocks
soil riddled with fine roots out of your eye-socket:
'Dad, can I take this home? Was it a man or a lady?'

IV

As regards public-sector cadavers, this year's
crop of corpses has been truly meagre.
The Lionel Longgones and Frank Fuckknowswhos
claim one another, each the other's "Own Dead".
Old gourmet of destruction, what a wry face you'd pull
to go through the same self-serchoice menu
for maybe the tenth time.
The populace has been dying
at the usual rate. Those who work, they in the end find bliss.
The latest thing is private mausolea. I find them less and less funny.
You gone, I have taken to browsing
through the deaths column more attentively
and reading the marble ID's they usually have
set up on the resting estates.
The servile soil produces its yews and cypresses,
bells ring, summoning us to follow someone,
on either side of the road there are fat snails
dragging their backs. The priest is about to utter
inanities, the two fat altar boys
fidget like bacon-rind sizzling in the pan.

God gives the sun no cloudy lining,
unmoved he hearkens to his feeble servant,
he beholds the pinky whiteness of women
swaddled in layers of black sweat down to their knickers,
listens to hoarse male singing, sees experts exchanging looks
as they pat into shape the flower-decked mound of earth. He's trying
to understand something of us. We, dispersing later,
buy savoury nibbles and the Evening News, our ladies'
fine moustaches get sticky with liqueur,
in the tram the widow wobbles, all puffed up –
a busy, white-cuffed paw (her consoler) groping toward her.
We stop off at the (Imitation) Marble Bride and have a few more.
It is all properly done.
I can't tell you much else, Péter. Nothing remarkable
– especially seen from there: through your specks of dust...

Christmas 1956

On the twenty-second, at a certain moment
(6.45 a.m.), I, a child of ill omen,
born between Joe S. and Jesus,
become thirteen. It's my last year
of Christmas being a holiday. There's
plenty to eat: the economy of scarcity
was to my Gran as the Red Sea: she passed over
with dry feet and a turkey. There's a present too –
for me: I control the market still – my one
cousin a mere girl, only four, and I
the last male of the line
(for the time being). Wine-soup, fish, there's everything,
considering we've just come up from the shelter –
where G.F. kept flashing a tommy-gun
with no magazine in it ('Get away, Gabe,' he was told,
'd'you want the Russkies after us?').
Gabe (he won't be hanged till it's lilac-time)
comes in wishing us a merry Christmas, there's no
midnight mass because of the curfew;
I concentrate on *Monopoly*, my present –
my aunt got it privately, the toyshops
not having much worth buying. My aunt has come,
in a way, to say goodbye: she's getting
out via Yugoslavia, but at the border (alas)
she'll be left behind, and so (in a dozen years about)
she'll be here when she has to die of spinal cancer.
Nobody knows how to play *Monopoly*, so
I start twiddling the knob on our Orion
wireless set, and gradually tune in
to London and America, like Mum in '44,
only louder: it's no longer forbidden – not yet.
The Christmas-tree decorations, known by heart,
affect me now rather as many years on
a woman will, one loved for many years.
In the morning, barefoot, I'm still to be found
rummaging through the *Monopoly* cards, inhaling
the smell of fir-tree and candles. I bring in
a plateful of brawn from outside, Gran
is already cooking, she squeezes a lemon,

slices bread to my brawn. I crouch on a stool
in pyjamas. There's a smell of sleep and holiday.
Grandad's coughing in what was the servant's room,
his accountant's body, toothpick-thin,
thrown by a fit of it from under the quilt,
Mother's about too, the kitchen is filling up
with family, and it's just as an observer
dropped in the wrong place that I am here:
small, alien and gone cold.

Christmas of '65

When Sára died, I didn't exactly move back home,
though where I *lived*, in which ARMPIT (as they say
in some quarters), it's truly hard to tell.
This home to which, as I say, I didn't move
on Christmas Eve '65 was in Buda (and still is,
a little uglier now): it was where
I wasn't living, but there I had my fill
of preserves made by my (then still living) Gran.
It was then I had a chat with my aunt's husband
(with what d'you call him, my great brother-in-law?),
who, as you can tell from what I've said, was alive still;
I chatted about the state of things, about the current
power relations (and he, too, in his modest way,
poor bloke, was a factor in all that, a constituent
of power, on the way to Chief Engineer).
Then something in blue flashed up on the TV
about Jesus and the manger (it was just around then
that the atheist state began playing the fool). In a word,
the baby was born in the light of a blue lamp
when topics for conversation were drying up
and the fruit had towered above its preserving juice
like a wrecked ship, its peel already wrinkling.
My Grandpa – well, by that time he'd been dead
for the past six months – would surely have fallen asleep
beside his homemade cherry-wine with soda
(a few drops would finish him off) and my Gran would have tried
in un-Christmassy spirit to wake him: 'Tony!
Don't snore at the table, you old bugger!' There were gifts even –
me, I think I got gloves. The women of the family
exchanged unopened skin lotions and creams
which would keep for the next occasion
when, having suffered repackaging after a shelved existence,
they'd transubstantiate into new gifts.
But Sára cannot be slapped back to life, with a little
mascara put on, or a frock, as a gift for men. So I,
probably wearing the freshly acquired gloves
(if I did get them that winter) set out at midnight
for a walk; my footsteps crunching through the snow
are perhaps retained in a Spirit-Ear's deep tunnels.

I set out from the said place toward Margit Bridge
to wade through the public near the Franciscan Church
as they trickled away after Mass, and stood for a long time
near the foot of the bridge, against which old icefloes shattered
        themselves,
their heads teeming with thaw.

Rhapsody

Why do we have to love you all the time?
You're like snowballs in our hands:
ready to melt, ready to be discarded.
A moment – you can't leave us in peace even that long.
You make us itch
in the crannies of the body,
as stars do the sky.

Mamma Gaby's dressing-gown flew wide open,
later she shut tight like water hit by a pebble.
'Bring me a pair of knickers from the cupboard,
you crazy ram. Who needs Vaseline when they've got you?'
And she bellowed like a French horn.

Ever since,
I've been after the thingamy between their legs
(strong-bellied woman, massive knees, peasant mother,
enormous breasts: the closing-down sale of a great body).
She's still alive. Quite old now.
I remember how, glimpsed in a mirror once,
she brushed her hand across her groin
and laughed, just laughed.

Much later:
another try – total disaster.
Complete resumption.
The modest lips flap open
like curtains on a backdrop
and one proceeds
as if in a long queue for the entrance desk.
at the pool, among coarse towels
and the smell of swimming-kit.

The Walk

Our slow walk out of life –
as the ad hoc company, in which we proceed, piles up,
as we lag behind, as we huddle closer together,
hurry ahead and stand aside – this walk
is worth our attention. Especially because
experiencing is entirely our own business –
it finds an end for itself in its own consummation:
both sting and sugar.

'The disposition to sting sweetly.'
That's how youth would have put it, long ago,
at a time when logic gave joy. At a certain age,
you don't go any more for that sort of thing.
Only things which, even unanalysed, are *something* –
a good sentence, a flawless pebble –
only they matter. You *may* ask, of course, What is "good"?
What is "flawless"? Sure. It's a question you *could* raise.
Only *I'm* not going to raise it.

Those coming after us
shove us forward, but also urge us to stay, as they drive us along.
Still, some dignity *can* be retained.
And more than just the appearance
of speed and direction. The right
to slow down, to double your pace, to wander off
can be exercised (although perhaps it is not
expedient to refer to it as a *right*).
Our walk, at any rate, is walk-like.
You just can't say that...Oh well, let's forget it.

But when you get to it, to the very end, to the point
where water falling becomes a waterfall –
the moment of rolling over roundedly –
the sheer slipperiness of the granite lip
is all you perceive. I'm putting this correctly: only that – up to a point.
Let us return to the road.
If our bemused state can squeeze a word
from unwordsworthiness, it isn't the road's fault.
Let us say: The road's interesting. It's beautiful.
(Really it is.) So let us walk and breathe.

Revenge

I can do whatever I want.
For instance, when we're making love,
I'll begin to shrink all over, proportionally,
and so contract out of you. I'll be tiny enough
to hide in your pubic hair. You'll look
all over the sheet for me, you'll diligently
comb the bedding, every last inch of it –
till finally you'll hear from your own belly
a giggle thin as a wire: there I shall be
running about, swinging my mini-manikin
and chirping 'Would you like to have me now?'

Electra

What *they* think is it's the twists and turns of politics
that keep me ticking; they think it's Mycenae's fate.
Take my little sister, cute sensitive Chrysothemis –
to me the poor thing attributes a surfeit of moral passion,
believing I'm unable to get over
the issue of our father's twisted death.
What do I care for that gross geyser of spunk
who murdered his own daughter! The steps into the bath
were slippery with soap – and the axe's edge too sharp.
But that this Aegisthus, with his trainee-barber's face,
should swagger about and hold sway in this wretched town,
and that our mother, like a venerably double-chinned old whore,
should dally with him simpering – everybody pretending
not to see, not to know anything. Even the Sun
glitters above, like a lie forged of pure gold,
the false coin of the gods!
Well, that's why! That's why! Because of disgust, because it all sticks
       in my craw,
revenge has become my dream and my daily bread.
And this revulsion is stronger than the gods.
I already see how mould is creeping across Mycenae,
which is the mould of madness and destruction.

To Imre Nagy

You were impersonal, too, like the other leaders,
bespectacled, sober-suited; your voice lacked
sonority, for you didn't know quite what to say

on the spur of the moment to the gathered multitude. This urgency
was precisely the thing you found strange. I heard you,
old man in pince-nez, and was disappointed,
not yet to know

of the concrete yard where most likely the prosecutor
rattled off the sentence, or
of the rope's rough bruising, the ultimate shame.

Who can say what you might have said
from that balcony? Butchered opportunities
never return. Neither prison nor death
can resharpen the cutting edge of the moment

once it's been chipped. What we can do, though, is remember
the hurt, reluctant, hesitant man
who nonetheless soaked up
anger, delusion
and a whole nation's blind hope,

when the town woke to gunfire
that blew it apart.

III

SINCE 1989

Cemetery Plot No.301

Let everything stay as it is!
With the carcasses from the Zoo?
Why, yes. Was their fate any different?
Was hanging any kinder than putting to sleep?
I cannot forget (when I say this,
I don't mean to threaten: it's the way I am:
I'm not able to forget).

On the other hand, what would I wish
for myself if I'd been – ha-ha! – hanged?
if I were to come back as a Stone Guest?
I'd wish at long last to be left in peace.
I shit on reverence. To these men
more mercy should've been shown when they were alive
(they should've been left alive). Now it's too late.

Against death there is no *remedium*.
No compensation for widows,
orphans, nations. I'm not interested
in the hangman's mate and his belated tears.
My eyes are dry. I need them for looking with.

Though actually there isn't much
to see – only, in the dusk
everything gets sharper:
a female body, a branch,
the downs of your face. I don't want
anything. Just to keep looking, no more.

Cold Peace

In the absence of peace, your plain man's mind might think
there will be war. There being no war,
it seems to your learnèd mind
that this is peace. But it is and will be neither.

Morning Coffee

I like the cold rooms of autumn, sitting
early in the morning at an open window,
or on the roof, dressing-gown drawn close,
the valley and the morning coffee glowing –
this cooling, that warming.

Red and yellow multiply, but the green
wanes, and into the mud the leaves
fall – fall in heaps,
the devalued currency of summer:
so much of it! so worthless!

Gradually the sky's
downy grey turns blue, the slight
chill dies down. The tide
of day comes rolling in –
in waves, gigantic, patient, barrelling.

I can start to carry on. I give myself up
to an impersonal imperative.

Sisyphus Steps Back

The age of intrepid idiots is upon us.
Fools or knaves? They're both at the same time.
I'm scared of understanding, and yet I laugh at it:
you can't stop a boulder once it's rolling back.

Daydreams

Into destruction I would bring
an order whole and classical.
Hope for the good? Out of the question.
Let me die invisible.

Sors bona nihil aliud. To
whoever digs my bones I send
a message: which is, Look how all
God's picture-images must end.

And no there cannot be a heaven,
or else there oughtn't to be one
for, if there were, this plague of love
would still (come what may) go on.

Nor do I want the obverse – hell –
though of that I've had, will have, my bit
(planks beneath the chainsaw wail).

For anything unready, yet
ready too, I lie in the sun:
let the redeeming nowhere come.

Smiley's Christmas

The pot still warm, the tea
was pleasantly drinkable.
The man who came in from the cold
felt awkward: how would things now be?
Might he never have to be cold again: was that possible?

Or would the whole thing ultimately
prove inextricable?
Would details slur, an error perhaps slip through?
He'd pretty soon be 50. And then 60?
By then a next time would be questionable.
Good hiding-places prove good traps as well.

But this one? This room too?

This too. Only, go through it like an auditor
through a bankrupt's fraudulent stack,
item by item, combing it as he must.
All that can save us now, all that can save,
is absolute distrust:
which, not afraid of letting up, not ever,
can just for that be kept warm without danger:
by a room externally
and internally a nice
strong cup of tea, with milk in it, and spice.

Something Unknown

Towards that something unknown
we'll come up against,
do we strive or are we driven?
the blue flower
of a new world, of new love,
enticing us, keeps flickering on and off:
will it lure us into a swamp?

How can you tell.
'Let it all be different now' –
the impulse, desire for that is no more than just:
so run-to-ground we were,
so pissed off we are!
As for self-pity, you can't object to that:
who else, ever at all, felt sorry for us?
And anyway,
we should ourselves
know best – if anyone does –
why we deserve
pity.

All the same, what lies ahead?
What lies ahead? I say.
It's the question
you can't evade
and can't answer.

As for the clot, it is
slowly, yes,
and also surely
swimming
towards the heart.

Elegy

When you are out, the flat is empty. I
just gasp for breath. The void or emptiness?
I'm all going and staying at once. Oh why
've you left me so much to my own devices?

On the hook, the counter-weight of myself
as I fish for the big catch. Will it come good?
I'm as consistent as a stack of wood.
That flying thing (look!), is it bird or stone?

I'm falling. Deeper and deeper I descend
into myself, but not so as to find
joy. It is surface, firm and flat, I yearn for.

This won't last long. Anyway, it will end
in death – but tell me, where am I now, which floor?
Let me slurp up – like an oyster from its shell –
my time with you, and my time without you as well.

Ideas and Dance-Music Records

'And where are our ideas
Of twenty years ago? Just being realised.'
ISTVÁN VAS

And what remains of István Vas?
I mean, apart from his writings,
but just now it's not of his writings
I wish to speak. Where's it gone, into what's it changed, his
    human stuff:
what we loved, the bodily dross, what's left when the spirit's been
    burned off?
God's servant the priest gave a balanced, an almost
precise consolation for loss.

But what shall I do with such comfort, who do not believe?
I who have only this single and singular life,
a bumpy, stony, muddy, swampy road of it
which leads, in the end, into the pit.
Or rather, another's hands in expert mode
board up one's "person" for one's last abode –
according to where on the scale of rank and wealth one happens to be,
one's coffin will be plain pine, or bronze, or mahogany.

So that 'we'll meet again up there' is something I can't believe in:
it's -270C in my notion of heaven.
The work, yes: there's no question of that not surviving.
But the man who drank red wine and smoked cigars – him I shall
    never again
meet in this stinking life, and still less in that yet more stinking
    death –
though our many stupidly unachieved encounters,
alas, how they ache with a sort of phantom pain,
just as legs, long since amputated, can start hurting again!

But never mind. We have to get used to this:
with time there'll be more and more people we miss.
After all, we have buried Pilinszky and Kálnoky;
how vile that a few of us should live on parasitically –
because for me, for a long time, survival or post-vival
has been bare-faced cheek, I wonder I have the face at all...
(My word-play, probably, wouldn't strike you as fun.)

But this whole poem, half out of tune, is just a dissonant drone:
a lot of sounds struggling to make a sound. Not for you.
You are no more. I do it for no reason, for myself, for I don't
        know who.
On a gramophone gone mad they keep going round and round –
worn-out ideas, old dance tunes, that scratchy sound.

Self-Portrait 1990

Strange spider:

empty
the menacing centre of attention.
Spokes and ribs
glisten unstirred.
Weave withstands storm,
there being no resistance:
because of the nigh-perfect
absence of sail.

As for himself, on his
lifeline-thread,
he keeps on yo-yoing
up – down
up – down

Epitaph

Death will come suddenly to a life ridden
into the ground. Decisions, achievements, successes
could still ripen inside it. But they won't.
Withered and still green, it perishes.

'If another life...' mumbles the wakeful sleep-machine
that's sensitised to make out any night noise.
There *is* no other life. You must learn how to lose.
(We luckily don't lose much, thanks to inflation.)

Purposeless almost, we keep up the grind
at what still lies ahead. Our gravestones won't
subside into rich soil. The world goes on
sweating, rotting, humming, as if behind
a slammed bar-door in the smell of food and smoke.

Credit Card

It's never a good idea
to rush things.
Annihilation included.
No good
ever comes of haste.
Therefore:
we stay alive.

In other words: we keep open
the purse of possibility.
We take death's million-pound note
and break it up
into the small change of life.

Or, not break it up exactly –
only present it.
For who on earth can give change
for such a fine, crisp deathnote?
But it's impressive. So
we can live on the never-never.

The General Bank of Death
guarantees everything.
So our balance always stands
at moral zero.

Mud

Things always were *instead* of something or other.
Of *what,* though, will remain a mystery.
Not of this world, nor hell, nor heaven either.
Not principles: fancies. Whim: not morality.

A whim? A fancy? No way. I went thud
like a rag ball that's drenched, heavy as stone,
when someone, not wishing to kick, tripped over me. Mud
is my soil and substance: dust waiting for rain.

I am one now with my soil and with my role.
What sets me apart is writing this, that's all:
so 'morning-evening-morning', let that come,

'i tak dalsje, und so weiter, and so on,
et cetera.' I'm different. Like others' sweat. Like the moon
rising. Da capo al segno. Ad libitum.

Options

You could say there's nothing left:
only an attempt to find your way
in the labyrinth of translation,
of the computer (and succeeding
in the end, though it never seems too
obvious that you have; more like
wandering down – in cyberspeak –
'invalid paths', in plain talk
impassable ones, or just untrodden).
You're left with the same old question
of what you are in reality. Options:
'both/and', 'either/or', 'neither/nor'.
Which leaves Mari. She *is* – if not
in *any* event. And though for me alone she is *ewige*,
she's also objectively, indisputably, *weibliche*.
She *is* – and that's the riddle which buoys me up.

Our Loves

Mostly those ad hoc shaggings on the side
filling the gaps between periods of boredom,
seducing one another's partners (mainly
to add some spice to the usual range of dishes
from the cafeteria at the sexual factory).
And then marriages lasting a decade and a half
that one was stuck in and forgot to get out of –
through absent-mindedness, bad housing problems
and the great big oh-it's-all-the-bloody-sameness.
Once, just to pass the time, I started counting
how many women I'd had altogether. I managed,
with the help of the name-day list in a calendar,
to *identify* over a hundred-and-fifty names.
That was OK. I still have an excellent memory
for names. Only I couldn't fit *faces* to them,
or even times and places and occasions.
So this now is my Aria of the Register,
which, lacking a Leporello, I've sung myself,
the *appropriate* Don Juan for a naff era.
It's one more thing I'm luckily too old for;
I'm only interested now in the state of my heart,
my liver, my prostate, my etcetera.
As for self-hatred, that's diminished too
(just a mask, by the way, for pride and ambition –
I simply could not come to terms with the fact
that I'm no better than those other shits,
my fellow-humans.) Now I'm beyond all that.
Now only there is nothing but the *now only*:
my wife, and what I think, and what I write.
And come to think of it, that's quite a lot.

Nonono

Right here, now, what isn't *is*.
It's the heyday of responsible fools
and responsible knaves. No! No! No!
I can't be doing with this, I won't have it!
Too many exclamation marks.
Question marks would be more appropriate.
Questionable now
is the sense of my own existence –
though suicide is no way out.
Or: "out" it certainly is, but it's no *way*.
It looks as if, after all, there's nothing at all to be after.
I did have a want once, one shared with others.
I don't want anything now.
I am quite alone.
But no, this is nonsense: I edit, I translate,
I have an effect. Therefore I'm a *factor* –
like it or not (i.e. I'm a coward).
I daren't plunge into depths of interior darkness.
I prefer to sit on the Abgrund Hotel terrace,
and I don't say No! No! No!
I swig at my beer and write poems,
I take pleasure in smoking a cigarette
(– well, even without pleasure, I still smoke it).
And then? Oh, the sands run. Life passes by.
Relatively speaking, this is still OK.
In the mean time,
everything's crumbling, falling apart. And I
simply can't say No! No! No!
Everything melts down into a N-n-n-yes.

Only Mari's Remained

Only Mari's remained – everything else has disappeared:
she is close to me, beating the air like some sort of bird.
A sparrow in the wet, a cheeky woodpecker,
or an ugly Balkan dove – in all her forms I like her.
She isn't basically a singing bird
yet it makes me so happy when she flings her arms out toward
me; if I can be her other half, in that case she,
she alone, is the answer to the problem why I am me.
(I mean, I am, but why should I *be* at all?)
That's why I courted you in the first place, my little Belle –
so that you'd be my Gothic castle and yet,
somewhere inside it, a Rococo banquet,
also a mystery play and a masked ball,
a jealous man who rants like hell;
an Othello of a husband, a little coquette –
a danger to touch her, so don't try that.
That's what I am and if, even so, I stay dear,
let me be the salted pretzel with your glass of beer.

Bosnia

fog, directions lost to sight,
mass graves, slaked lime, the smells
of carcasses in wells
and night, night, it's night

The Nothing Going On

Sunshine, leaves rustling, a light breeze,
a well-mown lawn and cherries ripening;
dogs, cats, pigeons
(and of course their respective droppings);
there is tripe for sale also
and the world economy balancing sooner or later.
There's everything and, what's more, it is such.
My lady's hair gleams golden. Mine, like my beard,
is silvery, as is proper for my years.
The shutter has not crashed down and the tin of fish
we managed to open with a household pneumatic drill.
As for the heat, it's a mere 35 in the shade.
We've a line (a stream-, more than one party-, a phone-). Look at it!
And yet, and yet! You can feel a growing lack.
But of what? What am I missing? There's the rub.
In the end I wish everybody would go to hell
and there's nothing I need in the world.
A bird to pull? A brief fling? Oh no! Not in this heat!
And anyway, why complicate life? Isn't what is
enough: the nothing that goes on?
I'm happy after all: I've a frisky wife full of juice
(sweats like a horse, frisks like a rocking-horse).
Events abroad occur in conformity
with the human race's global stupidity index.
I don't need possessions; my metabolism
is so good I manage to exist on air (plus a little beer).
And yet! And yet I've got the feeling
that NOTHING in the guise of a *grand process*
is going on. Of course, it's possible I can't see the wood for the trees
(and actually I can't see the trees either). Perhaps what I need
is to see an optician – that or a psychoanalyst.

Pop Song

The great work won't get written now: I'm through,
used up by all these years – what can I do?
I've shown myself no mercy and now see
in what I've done its sheer futility.

For in vain is all that energetic flow
if the machine's efficiency's too low.
And now it's much too late: 'cause nobody
can alter life or change it when past fifty.

No use lamenting or displaying rage –
awaiting me's the desert of old age.
Skin's getting wrinkly, gonna lose my teeth,
live a bit longer, then go meet my death.

It's already the 8th of November, which is great,
for we'll somehow manage till the end of the month
on the 55,000 we've got, and this and that
may well yet come our way, and if they don't
and we find that we can't manage, well even then
it's still possible to borrow, as
Auntie Mary and Uncle George
have a bank account, savings and monies due to them –
in a word, are *credit-worthy*. Oh yes, they've got
everything people of their age ought to have,
or in other words, which it's good to, so that
they've always got a something to dunk in their cocktails.
Cocktails I mention simply to give a hint
of the level of fee I now command,
my preference having once been for such refined
gut-rot as KREPKAYA VODKA, which is fierce
as red-hot chilli peppers. But where is it now?
Ah why did you collapse and fall apart,
oh boundlessly deep and purest source of vodka,
great USSR? How *could* you do this to me,
oh *Free Republics United in Alliance*?
Who will now provide our daily shot
of mind-blasting mad-cow? Where today can you get
a good enough DVESTY GRAMM to knock your brains out? And
       then me:
where is the 28 year-old, quite worn for his age,
who waves back from the TU-134
to his wife and his lover (his second wife-to-be)
and then, jamming his bum into the bone-crushing seat,
pulls out a bottle of STOLICHNAYA VODKA
and a packet of *Dunhills* bought for the occasion,
waits for the *No Smoking* to switch off, lights his fag,
swigs from the bottle with calm deliberation and, looking bored,
keeps flicking, as if he knew Russian, through his IZVESTIYA?
And his fellow-passengers? Twenty middle-rank functionaries,
all in plum-blue state-manufactured suits and all
totally pissed. (It's at this point he begins
to develop the habit of forgetting Hungarian

if there happen to be Hungarians on board.)
But I now return to the first person singular,
for sufficient indication has now been given
as to how alienated from that one-time self
I have become. Till we get to the right altitude, the flight
is entertaining – the plane keeps falling steeply in air-pockets. But once
above the clouds – smooth boredom, as over a frozen lake.
(With me, flying is just like everything else: a couple of minutes
and I'm used to it: I've got a new routine.) At last
we hit the 'Hungarian concrete' of SHEREMETYEVO airport –
I'm quoting our Uncle Johnnie, now deceased.
We crowd into a shitty-old ramshackle bus. It moves like a snail
to passport-control, where under the semi-transparent smoke-glazed
            window
I, too, slide my passport. The guard, a Baltic Slav with piercing eyes,
takes a good look to see if I am me. YOB TVAYU MAT', SASHENKA!
Believe your own eyes, will you! (Of course, it's possible
he'd read too much *Lukács* – that *Georg von Lukacs* who long ago had
            said:
'The eye, the organ of sight, can hinder your seeing clearly.'
[Vulgo: 'The cock, your organ of fucks, can hinder your fucking.'])
All right, let's go, let's go! Out of here! Even
out of this poem the nightmare is evoked in. At last. Aaargh!
I'm outside in the arrival lounge. And there, there's a board held up
and on it, in huge letters, PETRI. BOZHE MOY, BOZHE MOY.
There's also, beside my name, a skinny lady, she who's to guide me
through the ominous bowels of the USSR, my Virgilia.
We get into a black CHAYKA, a reception befitting a diplomat,
and all that is missing 's the convoy of cars and the escort
with sirens blowing to secure the route. Even so, it's impressive.
Considering the traffic, which is like Tehran (cars, motorbikes,
bi- and tri-cycles, carts, hand-carts, donkey-carts) we still arrive
at TCHAIKOVSKAYA PLOSHAD', then enter the GOSTINNICA PEKIN.
The architecture's depressing, tacky Stalin-Baroque,
a bit like Lomonosov University, only smaller
(there are dozens like it in Moscow). There's a DEZHURNAYA on duty,
a kind of hotel servant, but more like a gaoler: she speaks
not a word but Russian, a fat-calved slovenly slag, a thick unfriendly
            cow.
My room has an enormous double-bed with a purple cover, a pseudo-
            rococo desk,

and a brass table-lamp with a glass globe, half of it made to look like
       a frilly mauve silk bonnet.
Well, that's enough. Of the room, I mean. I tell my escort I'd like
       a drink.
Unfortunately, in all six of the hotel restaurants and bars, right now,
they're throwing a huge reception, closed to the public. Well, in
       that case, what about a pub?
Pubs do exist. When we get out on to the square, my escort takes me
to a charming alley with six lanes for cars. And I can confirm: there
       are indeed pubs. I must admit.
I am truly confused by the choice. I plunge into the first. Yeah!
       This is to my taste.
You can cut the smoke. It smells of beer, vodka, urine, and herrings
       with onions.
I elbow and shoulder my way through, like a tank (it's the custom:
       no IZVINITE, no POZHALUSTA –
say that and at best they laugh at you, though they might well
       push your face in
or knee you hard in the balls) and I only have to say tersely, DVESTY
       GRAMM,
and at once there's a big glass before me – you can tell it's not
       mineral water.
And suddenly out of the blue, like a fairy godmother, Anya
is there with some oily gherkins and a phone number. She hands
       them over – and disappears.
I take a big gulp. Everyone round me is pissed like a cunt, all of
       them singing or howling.
They slap me on the back and embrace me. 'VENGRYA KHOROSHO!'
       One round, then another.
They pay, I pay. I am waltzing with Mother Moscow. My head in her
       cleavage,
her sweetish smell of KRASNAYA MOSKVA eau-de-cologne gets into
       my lungs. Everything's fine.
Now I am happy.

A Recognition

1

The weather-beaten captain of a small riverboat,
I used to navigate history's local route.
I have come ashore now. Not through desert, but duty.
Here I am and the whole thing's beyond me.

2

The epoch expired like a monstrous predator.
My favourite toy's been snatched.

NOTES

22-23. By an Unknown Poet from Eastern Europe, 1955: The date is significant. Petri is thinking back to the darkest days of the Stalinist regime in the early 1950s.

28-29. To S.V.: Addressed to Petri's friend and fellow-poet, Szabolcs Várady. The opening stanza refers to the spectacular Adam Clark suspension bridge, which spans the Danube in the centre of Budapest. One the mountainous Buda side, the road over the bridge leads directly into a tunnel, the far end of which is visible from the bridge.

32. Gratitude: The public holiday referred to is probably the anniversary of the Soviet liberation of Hungary, 4 April 1945. This used to be celebrated annually with a salute of guns.

34-36. Eternal Monday: Some of the epithets for the days of the week are taken from a Hungarian nursery rhyme. Others are traditional, notably those (like Ash Wednesday) that come from the Church's calendar.

37. Gloss on a Discussion: The dedicatee is a Hungarian critic, who has written a perceptive study of Petri's work.

The use of German in this poem is connected with Petri's continuing quarrel with German philosophy. There is, however, a striking contrast between coarse colloquialisms and philosophical terms. *Repression* and *Toleranz* are terms from the writings of Herbert Marcuse, whose theory of 'repressive tolerance' was fashionable among student radicals in the 1960s. *Nebich* is a Yiddish colloquialism roughly translatable as 'big deal'. High philosophy or theology immediately returns with *Vollendete Sündhaftigkeit* – 'perfect sinfulness' – while *alle beide stinken* is coarsely colloquial again – 'both stink'.

46. Night Song of the Personal Shadow: The last lines evoke the end of the Second World War in Budapest, when the Hungarian Fascists executed Jews and deserters by lining them up on the embankments of the Danube and shooting them into the river.

44-45. The Under-Secretary Makes a Statement: Written between August 1980 and December 1981, shortly after the emergence of the Solidarity trade union in Poland and before the imposition of martial law. The *zloty* is the Polish currency.

52-55. In Memoriam: Péter Hajnóczy: Hajnóczy (1942–81) was a Hungarian writer noted for his experimental prose (e.g. the short novel *Death Rides Out from Persia,* 1979).

'Each other's "Own Dead"': Petri parodies a formula used in official announcements of death – e.g. 'The Party regards X as its own dead and takes responsibility the funeral expenses'.

56-57. Christmas 1956: i.e. two months after the uprising. 'Between Joe S. and Jesus': Joseph Stalin was also born in December. *Monopoly:* in Hungary the game is called *Capitaly.*

63. Electra: This version of the Agamemnon story is partly concerned with the love-affair between Mother Hungary (Clytemnestra) and the smooth master of compromise, János Kádár (Aegisthus). Kádár was Hungarian Communist leader from 1957 to 1989.

64. To Imre Nagy: Nagy was Prime Minister of the short-lived revolutionary Government, October–November 1956. The poem telescopes two events: Nagy's speech from the balcony of the Parliament building in Budapest on 23 October, when the uprising began, and his execution by order of the Kádár regime in June 1958. The last two lines refer to the second Soviet attack on the Government and its supporters, 4 November 1956.

66. Cemetery Plot No.301: When Imre Nagy and his colleagues were hanged, their bodies were immediately dumped in a cemetery on the outskirts of Budapest. Their grave, which was unmarked, was in plot no.301. In June 1989, the events of 1956 were officially recognised as a 'popular uprising' and the bodies of Nagy and his co-defendants were exhumed for a state funeral. They were then reburied in plot no.301. When the graves were first opened, it was found that animal bones from a nearby zoo had been buried along with the humans.

70. Daydreams: The Latin phrase is the motto of Count Miklós Zrínyi, a 17th-century poet and general. It means, roughly, 'Good fortune is all you need.'

71. Smiley's Christmas: This is George Smiley from John Le Carré's spy novels, though in Le Carré 'the spy who came in from the cold' was Alec Leamas.

74-75. Ideas and Dance-Music Records: An elegy for István Vas (1910-1991), an outstanding poet and translator, who was one of the young Petri's mentors. Vas (pronounced 'Vosh') wrote a poem with the same title as this. János Pilinszky and László Kálnoky were celebrated poets, both of whom died in the 1980s. The temperature -270° Celsius should be read 'minus two-seventy C' for the sake of the rhythm.

79. Mud: '*i tak dalsje*' and '*und so weiter*' are, respectively Russian and German for the English 'and so on'. 'Da capo al segno' (Italian): 'from the start to here' (a musical expression). 'Ad libitum' (Latin): 'as you please', 'at your pleasure'.

80. Options: *ewige* (German for 'eternal'); *weibliche* (German for 'feminine'). The reference is to Goethe's concept of the eternal feminine in *Faust*.

82. Nonono: *Abgrund* is German for 'abyss' or 'precipice'.

85. The Nothing Going On: 'a mere 35' (degrees Celsius).

87-89. *from* **The Great Journey:** This is the first section of a long poem, the rest of which has not been published yet. It includes several Russian words and phrases, which are translated among the following notes:

line 3: 55,000 Hungarian forints was about £160 in 1998. The average monthly income in Hungary was 35,000 forints.

line 24: Vodka is measured in grams in Russia. Two hundred grams is a double.

line 33: Izvestiya was a well-known Soviet newspaper.

line 48: Uncle Johnnie: János Kádár.

line 52: YOB...SASHENKA: 'Fuck your mother, Alex!'

line 54: Georg (György) Lukács, the Hungarian philosopher and literary critic, wrote most of his work in German. The 'von' reminds us of his upper-class origins and stands in ironic contrast to his Marxist ideology.

line 60: BOZHE MOY: 'Oh, my God.'

line 68: TCHAIKOVSKAYA...PEKIN: Tchaikovsky Square, Beijing Hotel.

line 71: DEZHURNAYA: A female attendant on duty.

line 83: IZVINITE...POZHALUSTA: 'Excuse me', 'please'.

line 90: VENGRYA KHOROSHO: 'Hungary is good!'

line 92: KRASNAYA MOSKVA: Red Moscow – a brand name.

Printed in the USA
CPSIA information can be obtained
at www.ICGtesting.com
JSHW082223140824
68134JS00015B/704

9 781852 245047